the greatest gift of all

*An Inspirational Press Book
for Children*

Story by KIMBERLY RINEHART

Illustrations by GEORGIA RETTMER

First Inspirational Press edition published in 1997.

Inspirational Press
A division of BBS Publishing Corporation
386 Park Avenue South
New York, NY 10016

Inspirational Press is a registered trademark of BBS Publishing Corporation.

Published by arrangement with it takes two®, inc.

Library of Congress Catalog Card Number: 97-71143
ISBN: 0-88486-185-6
Printed in China

the greatest gift of all

the innkeeper offered...

a bed of hay.

the donkey offered . . .

a strong back.

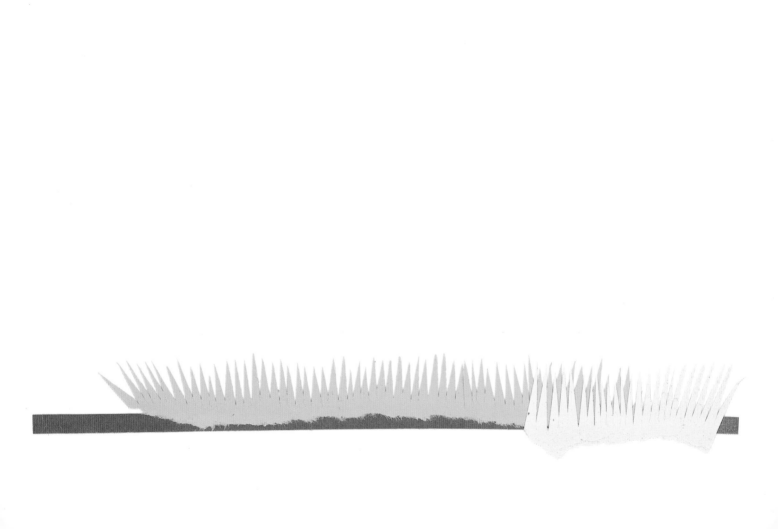

the cow offered...

fresh, white milk.

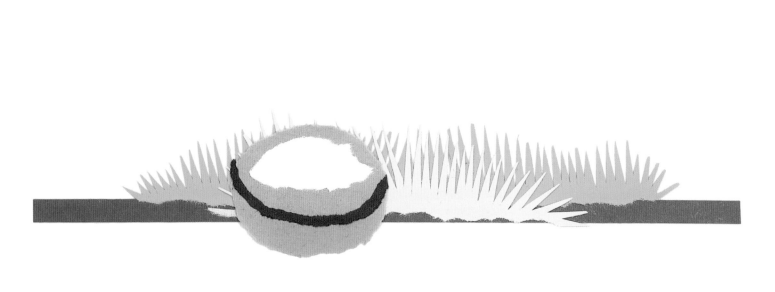

the sheep offered . . .

the warmth of their wool.

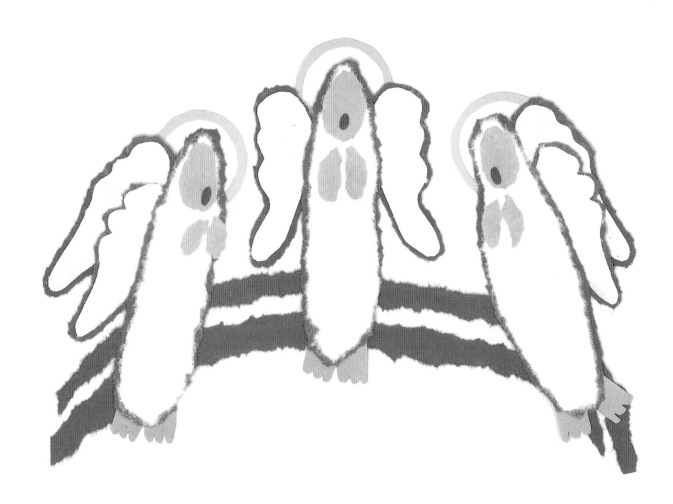

the angels offered...

the gift of song.

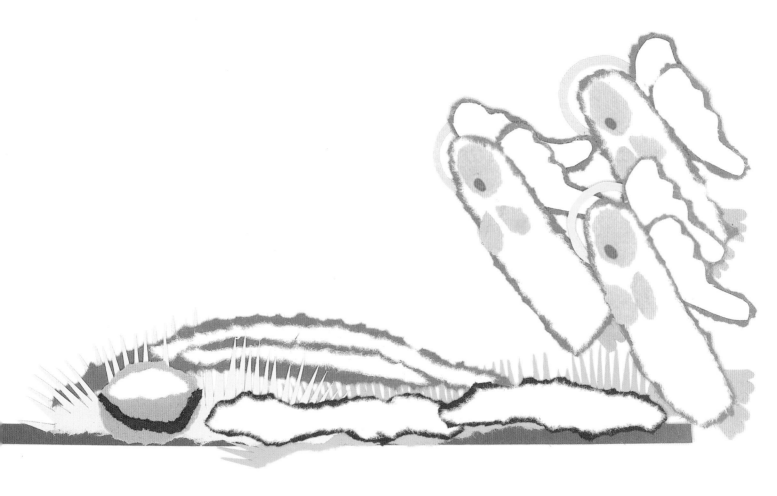

the star offered...

its guiding light.

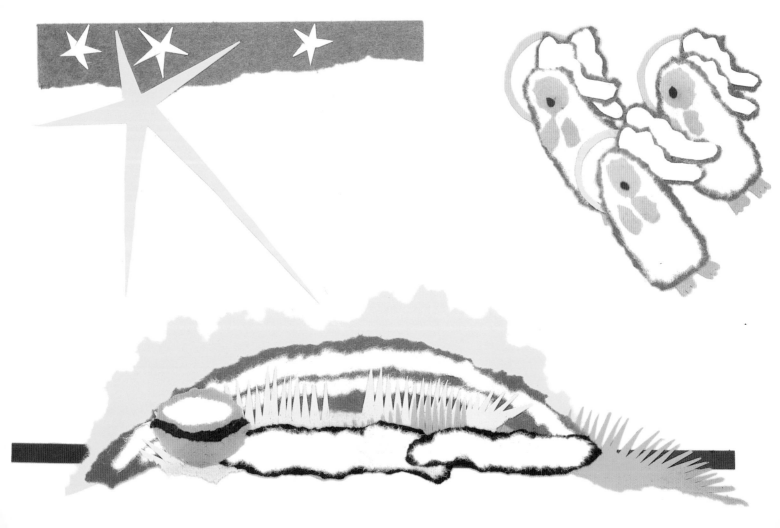

the shepherds offered...

their humble hearts.

the wisemen offered....

gold and precious gifts.

the father offered...

patience and kindness.

the mother offered . . .

love and care.

but isn't it a wonder...

that the tiny helpless baby offered...

In those days Caesar Augustus issued a decree that a census should be taken of the entire Roman world. (This was the first census that took place while Quirinius was governor of Syria.) And everyone went to his own town to register. So Joseph also went up from the town of Nazareth in Galilee to Judea, to Bethlehem the town of David, because he belonged to the house and line of David. He went there to register with Mary, who was pledged to be married to him and was expecting a child. While they were there, the time came for the baby to be born, and she gave birth to her firstborn, a son. She wrapped him in cloths and placed him in a manger, because there was no room for them in the inn. And there were shepherds living out in the fields nearby, keeping watch over their flocks at night. An angel of the Lord appeared to them, and the glory of the Lord shone around them, and they were terrified. But the angel said to them, "Do not be afraid. I bring you good news of great joy that will be for all the people. Today in the town of David a Savior has been born to you; he is Christ the Lord. This will be a sign to you: You will find a baby wrapped in cloths and lying in a manger." Suddenly a great company of the heavenly host appeared with the angel, praising God and saying, "Glory to God in the highest, and on earth peace to men on whom his favor rests." When the angels had left them and gone into heaven, the shepherds said to one another, "Let's go to Bethlehem and see this thing that has happened, which the Lord has told us about." So they hurried off and found Mary and Joseph, and the baby, who was lying in the manger. When they had seen him, they spread the word concerning what had been told them about this child, and all who heard it were amazed at what the shepherds said to them. But Mary treasured up all these things and pondered them in her heart. The shepherds returned, glorifying and praising God for all the things they had heard and seen, which were just as they had been told.

Luke 2:1-20 (NIV)